No Job Is Too Big for Frannie B. Miller

FRANKLY, FRANNIE

Here Comes the... Trouble!

by AJ Stern

illustrated by Doreen Mulryan Marts

Grosset & Dunlap
An Imprint of Penguin Group (USA) Inc.

For the entire Stern-Stuart clan.
Otherwise known as my family.—AJS

Thanks as always to everyone at Penguin: Francesco Sedita, Bonnie Bader,
Scottie Bowditch, and my editor, Jordan Hamessley, and also, of course,
to Doreen Mulryan Marts, who draws Frannie just like I'd pictured her.
Your support and enthusiasm is unparalleled! To Julie Barer, who negotiates like
nobody's business and to my family and friends for support. Special thanks go to
Esther and Richard Eder in whose house I wrote this and to Frances Eder whose
daily word count check-ins became my favorite time of day. Thanks to Luke Eder
for introducing me to the island of Vinalhaven, where I wrote this book. And of
course to my nieces and nephews: Maisie, Mia, Lili, Adam, and Nathan, without
whom I'd have lost touch long ago with the band and beauty of kid linguistics.—AJS

GROSSET & DUNLAP
Published by the Penguin Group
Penguin Group (USA) Inc., 375 Hudson Street, New York, New York 10014, USA
Penguin Group (Canada), 90 Eglinton Avenue East, Suite 700, Toronto,
Ontario M4P 2Y3, Canada (a division of Pearson Penguin Canada Inc.)
Penguin Books Ltd., 80 Strand, London WC2R 0RL, England
Penguin Group Ireland, 25 St. Stephen's Green, Dublin 2, Ireland
(a division of Penguin Books Ltd.)
Penguin Group (Australia), 250 Camberwell Road, Camberwell, Victoria 3124,
Australia (a division of Pearson Australia Group Pty. Ltd.)
Penguin Books India Pvt. Ltd., 11 Community Centre,
Panchsheel Park, New Delhi—110 017, India
Penguin Group (NZ), 67 Apollo Drive, Rosedale, Auckland 0632, New Zealand
(a division of Pearson New Zealand Ltd.)
Penguin Books (South Africa) (Pty.) Ltd., 24 Sturdee Avenue,
Rosebank, Johannesburg 2196, South Africa

Penguin Books Ltd., Registered Offices: 80 Strand, London WC2R 0RL, England

Text copyright © 2012 by AJ Stern. Illustrations copyright © 2012
by Penguin Group (USA) Inc. All rights reserved. Published by Grosset & Dunlap,
a division of Penguin Young Readers Group, 345 Hudson Street, New York, New York 10014.
GROSSET & DUNLAP is a trademark of Penguin Group (USA) Inc. Printed in the U.S.A.

Library of Congress Control Number: 2012009702

ISBN 978-0-448-45752-9 (pbk)   10 9 8 7 6 5 4 3 2 1
ISBN 978-0-448-45753-6 (hc)   10 9 8 7 6 5 4 3 2 1

ALWAYS LEARNING   **PEARSON**

CHAPTER

My best friend Elliott's mom was getting married in two weeks. I was going to be the flower girl. If you don't already know about this job, it's very important, indeed. It was one of the best jobs I've ever been offered. It means you're in charge of all the flowers! That's nearly as important as being the actual bride, and that is not an opinion.

Even though I am not a very **flowerish** type of person, I *am* a very in-chargish type of person. This is a for instance of why I couldn't wait for the in-chargish part of things to start. And, although it was the first wedding I'd ever been to, I already knew it would be the best wedding I'd ever been to.

Elliott hadn't been to a wedding, either, and until this morning, he had been excited, too. My mom and I picked him up on the way to school. As soon as he got in the car, I knew something was wrong. He was very pale and had the most worrified expression on his face. He scooted over and whispered to me, "George wants to talk to me after school!" His eyeballs were very nervousing.

George was going to be Elliott's stepfather. Elliott is my best friend in the world, so I know a lot of very important things about him. One very important thing is he does not like to wait for things to happen. He just wants them to happen. So if someone says they need to talk to him later, his eyeballs begin to **nervousify**. This is because in the time between, Elliott **worries his entire face off**. I guess my mom knows this, too, because she looked in the rearview mirror at him and **scooched** a very small smile up on her face. I'm really smart about scooched-up, very small smile faces.

"What do you think George wants to talk to me about?" Elliott whisper-asked.

"I don't know, but I don't think it's anything bad," I told him.

"Shhh!" he said, and then nudged his chin toward my mom. He didn't want her to hear any of this. Just in case it turned out to be something very **tragical**.

"Maybe he wants to make you a flower boy," I suggested.

Elliott **crunkled** his face up at this. I did not appreciate this crunkle because I was going to be a flower girl! I was very **offendified**!

"What if he says I'm not invited to the wedding?!"

"Why in the worldwide of America would he say that?" I asked.

Elliott shrugged.

When we got to school, we jumped out of the car and waved good-bye to my mom. Elliott was so **distractified**, he walked down the wrong hall!

In science he was my lab partner.

We were doing experiments about floating eggs. Everyone had two bowls of warm water in front of them.

"You put in two tablespoons of salt, and I'll stir it," I told him, pointing to one of the bowls.

"What if George changed his mind and doesn't want to marry my mom anymore?" Elliott asked, sitting down on a stool, holding the empty measuring spoons.

"No, my inside guts are telling me that's not right," I told him. I took the spoons from him and scooped out two tablespoons of salt and put them in one of the bowls.

"Then what? What could it be?!" Elliott cried out. Everyone turned to look at him, which was very embarrassifying. His face turned into

a pomegranate. That's how red he was.

"Look, Elliott!" I said. "One egg is floating, and the other egg sank!"

Elliott looked at the eggs, but I could tell his eyeballs were not focused on them at all. He was not easy to distractify when he was already distractified.

"I just don't know what it could be," he said.

I didn't, either, actually and as a matter of fact. But I didn't think it was bad. If it WAS bad, my inside guts would have told me. My inside guts are very smart about feelings.

"My dad says that it's a waste of time to worry about things you can't control," I told Elliott. My dad is really smart about sayings.

"Why?" Elliott wanted to know.

"Because it's going to happen one way or the other. Worrying isn't going to change a thing," I explained.

"I guess that makes sense," he said.

"It does indeed and very certainly," I told him. After all, my dad was the one who said it, and he is never wrong about a saying.

"But I'm still worried!" he told me.

When the end of the day finally got here, Elliott and I went downstairs together. Our mothers were in the hall waiting for us.

"Where's George?" Elliott asked his mom.

"That's the hello I get?" His mom, Julie, asked, **pretend-offendified**.

"Hi, Mom, where's George?"

"You're all coming to our house

to do some wedding preparations," my mom told us.

"George will meet us there. He wants to talk to you," Elliott's mom said.

"I know." Elliott groaned and put his hand on his stomach.

We got in the car and drove to my house. The closer we got, the worse Elliott looked.

"I'm sure it will be fine," I told him.

"Will you come with me when it happens?" he asked.

I nodded, feeling a lot of **pride-itity** that he asked. "Indeed and nevertheless, I will," I told him. That is the **most official and grown-up** way a person can say yes.

CHAPTER

The second we walked through the front door, Elliott flung his head all around the place.

"Where's George?" he asked.

"He's coming soon. Don't worry," Julie said.

She and my mom went into the living room to look at Julie's big wedding binder. It was filled with magazine cutouts of wedding cakes and flowers and candles and things.

Julie wouldn't show us a picture of the dress because **apparently and nevertheless** it's bad luck to show the dress to anyone before the wedding day. This is a fact I didn't know about.

A fact I *did* know about was that I was going to be a flower girl and my mom was going to be a bridesmaid. Even though she had the word *bride* in her job, she was not getting married. Plus and besides, she was already married to my dad! My dad was going to be a groomsman, and even though he had the word *groom* in his job, he wasn't getting married, either. It was all very **confusifying**, which is a for instance of why kids don't get married.

Julie and George's wedding was going to be at an apple orchard. I thought that was a very good idea, indeed. For one thing, it would smell **apple-icious**. The orchard had a barn part, and that's where we were going to celebrate after the actual getting married part. My mom's job was to help Julie with whatever things she needed. My mom is very **helpfulish** that way.

I stood looking over my mom's shoulder at the book, while Elliott paced back and forth behind me. He sat down, but was **jittering** his legs so much, he got back up to pace again.

"Do you know what you two could do while you wait for George?" Julie said to us.

"What?" I wanted to know.

She pointed to a small cardboard box.

"You can make the place cards. You have to print very carefully, though.

The list of people is on top of all the place cards. Do you want to do that?" she asked us.

"Yes!" I cried and raced over to the box. Elliott looked out the window, shrugged, and said, "I guess."

As soon as we opened the box, the doorbell rang and Elliott raced to get it. I got started on the place cards.

"George!" Elliott cried as soon as the door opened.

"What a nice welcome committee," George said to Elliott. He came in, my mother took his coat, and Elliott stared at him.

"Is there a place where Elliott and I can talk privately?" he asked my smiling mom.

"Of course! How about in the library?" She pointed behind him.

"Perfect. Elliott, may I borrow you
for a minute?"

Elliott nodded yes and asked, "Can
Frannie come?"

"Frannie will wait right here for you," he said and went to the library. Elliott followed behind, and I stayed in the living room. Now I was the one who was **worrified**! Why in the worldwide of America did it need to be *private*?!

I paced back and forth waiting for them to come out. Then I sat down and **jittered** my legs. Then I stood up again and paced. Finally, they came out of the room. When I saw Elliott's face, I knew it was good news. George patted me on the head as he passed me in the living room.

"Well?" I asked Elliott.

"He wants me to be the best man!" he told me.

"WOW!" I said. My stomach got a little bit **jealousish**. I wanted to be the best girl. I was the best at a lot of things. Not anything I could think of right that second, but the feeling in my guts told me I was right. "That's very exciting."

"I know," he said. Elliott smiled his face all over the place.

When we went back into the living room, Elliott jumped up and down in front of his mom, who was also smiling her face off!

"Guess what?" Elliott practically shouted.

Julie scrunched her face up into her best "hmmmm . . . let me think" face before saying, "I give up! Wait, wait! Are you going to be the BEST MAN?"

"YES!!! How in the world did you even know that?!" Elliott was so surprisified, and Julie laughed and hugged him.

"Because George and I discussed it, and it's something we didn't even have to think one second about. I'm thrilled, Elliott. I couldn't have asked for a better best man." She gave him the biggest best man squeeze and said,

"How about we go out and celebrate?"

That's when I started jumping up and down, too. "Yay!!!"

"It'd be a good time for us to explain everyone's role at the wedding, too," my mom said. She was very **practicalish**.

Elliott ran to get George, and we put our jackets on and raced out to the car. It was not every single second we got to go out to eat! This was very **excitifying**, indeed.

While we were sitting down at our table waiting for our french fries, Julie told us how a wedding works.

"First the reverend, George, and Elliott will walk out and stand at the altar. Then the groomsmen and the bridesmaids walk down the aisle. Then the flower girl"—that's when everyone

looked at me and smiled, and I blushed
my cheeks off—"and then, me and my
father," Julie said.

"I walk out right BEFORE you do?"
I asked.

"That's right," she said.

"That is very important, indeed,"
I announced.

"It really is. A flower girl is a big
job," my mom said.

"Almost as important as being a
bride," I said, nodding yes at myself.

Julie, George, and my mom laughed.
George said, "Well, not quite, but it's a
very big job."

"Being the best man is also a very
important job," Julie said. We all looked
at Elliott, who blushed his face off, too.

"The biggest," George said. Elliott
smiled, but I could see a little bit of

worry swim up to his face.

Even if my job wasn't the biggest, I still liked everything about it. Except for the dress part. Julie had already picked it out, and when she showed me a picture of it, I had to pretendify that I liked it. If a field of flowers **exploded** all over a dress, that is a for instance of what it looked like. **However and nevertheless**, although I did not appreciate all the flowers, I did appreciate that I got to walk down an aisle. Even if it was really a grassy, apple orchard aisle. I had to do it very slow, too. Unlike when you are a model, which was a job I once had.

When you're a model, you have to walk very **fastly** up and down, and you're only on the stage for three seconds. Being a model is a very fast job, so I don't prefer it. I like to be onstage for longer than three seconds. Also flower girls are very important because they come out right before the bride.

CHAPTER

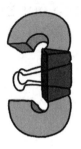

The next day, Elliott and I were in the cafeteria eating our lunches, except Elliott had barely even tasted his spaghetti.

"What's the matter, Elliott?" I asked him.

"Well," he said slowly. "You know how I'm the best man at the wedding?"

I nodded yes, because it was **a scientific fact** that I did know.

"The problem is that I don't know

exactly what that means," he admitted.

It was a very good thing that I was his friend.

"It's easy," I told him. "You just have to be the best at everything and make sure nothing goes wrong!"

That's when his eyeballs almost fell into his spaghetti.

"I don't know how to do that!" he said.

"Sure, you do!" I told him.

"I do?" he asked.

"Well, I don't know for a scientific fact, but it doesn't seem so hard to me," I said.

"But I don't even know what I'm supposed to be the best at!" Elliott said, getting very **frusterated**.

This was very **trickish**. Since I had never been to a wedding before, I wasn't really sure, either.

"Well, let's see. There's the job of best dancer. The job of best aisle walker-downer. The best eater of the cake, the best maker of speeches, the best at not laughing at the wrong times. Also, you have to make sure that nothing goes wrong. That's part of being the best man."

Elliott looked a little bit green.

"It's not a big deal, Elliott. I can help you. You just have to make sure that everyone shows up and that the band remembers all their songs. That the cake is delicious. That the flowers don't die. That it's a sunny day. That there are enough seats for everyone. Stuff like that," I said.

"But I don't know how to do ANY of that, Frannie! I just don't know how!!"

Elliott was starting to really freak

out now. I could tell because he pushed his plate of spaghetti away.

"I'll help you!" I offered.

"You will?"

"Yes! I'll be the wedding planner!" I told him.

"What's that?" he asked.

"Someone who plans weddings!" I answered.

"Do you know how to do that?" he asked me, which was very **offendifying**!

"Of course I know how to do that! I have planned a **hundredteen** weddings!" I cried.

"You have?" he asked.

"Well, not in real life, but I could have if a **hundredteen** people had asked me to," I explained.

"When can you start?"

"Right now!" I answered.

"Great," he said, unzipping his backpack and pulling out a piece of loose-leaf paper and a pen. It turns out that being a wedding planner is not as easy as it looks. There is a lot of work to do.

"Let's write down everything that happens at a wedding," Elliott said.

"Okay," I agreed.

Since neither of us had ever been to a wedding, we were both a little **stumpified**.

"There is a dress," I said, writing it down.

"There's a ring," Elliott said. "And a cake."

"People make speeches," I said.

"A band plays," Elliott said.

"People are in the wedding, up in the

front," I said, writing that down, too.

Our friend Elizabeth came over and sat down.

"What are you doing?" she asked.

"Planning a wedding," I said.

"Oh, I just love weddings!" she said. "My favorite is the vows part."

Elliott and I looked at each other, and I wrote down the word *vows*.

"Is this for your mom's wedding?" Elizabeth asked.

Elliott nodded.

"Did she have a bridal shower?" Elizabeth asked Elliott.

"I don't know," he said. "I suppose so." He looked at me for the answer, but I had no idea what the answer was because I had no idea what she was talking about. What made a shower a bridal shower and not just a regular shower?

Elizabeth asked questions about the ring and the dress and the honeymoon. I wrote down *honeymoon*.

I did not know there was so much to

a wedding. I was writing down words as **fastly** as I could to keep up with Elizabeth. I tried to close my brain off so Elliott couldn't read my brain. I did not want him to read how **worrified** I was getting. But I don't think I closed it fastly enough, because when I looked up, he was staring at me with eyeballs that said "I just read every last one of your brain notes."

It is not an opinion that being the best at everything IS harder than it looks.

CHAPTER

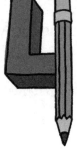

Elliott and I were not expecting
our moms to pick us up again, so we
were **surprisified** to see them waiting
outside after school.

"What are you doing here?" I asked.

"We're going to the wedding
planner's office and thought you'd
like to come with us."

Elliott and I looked at each other,
and our eyeballs almost fell out of our
heads at the exact same time!

"WEDDING PLANNER!?" I shoutified. That's when I got a bad day feeling on my skin. If Julie already had a wedding planner, then *I* couldn't be the wedding planner! There can't be two of everything!

"Yes. Isn't that exciting?" my mom asked.

"I suppose so," I said, slunking into the car. I was not excitified for someone else to do my job.

"I thought you would be more excited than that!" my mom said. "They have offices!"

I had to smile at that part. I love jobs that have offices.

"I didn't know that wedding planners had offices," I said.

"They do. Susan's is very big, too," Julie told us.

The **disappointment puddle** at my feet dried up at that news. After all, offices made me very happy, so I was starting to feel a *little* bit better!

Susan's office was right outside of Chester. You will not even believe your ears about how big her office was. And you will also not **believe your ears** about how many assistants Susan had! She had **twentyteen** assistants! And everyone, even Susan, carried a clipboard! I love clipboards! I love offices that have **twentyteen** assistants who all carry clipboards! Being a wedding planner was the best job in the world.

The office also had corkboards all over the walls. There were magazine cutouts of dresses, flowers, barns, candles, invitations, rings—everything you can possibly imagine was pinned to it. There were the hugest binders I've ever seen piled on desktops and a machillion pieces of fabric all over the place. I wanted to work in this office very badly.

Susan knew where every single thing was. **A for instance** of what I mean is that when Julie brought up candles, Susan pulled out the exact right book, opened it to the exact right page, and pointed to the exact right candles that Julie wanted. There were a lot of little sticky notes everywhere, and that's how I knew that Susan's books were really important. If you want to know if something is important, you should always look for a sticky note. I needed to get sticky notes. I needed to get a clipboard. *Clipboards and sticky* *notes. Clipboards and sticky notes.*

I am always very interested to know whether someone is good or bad at her job. This is a very important thing to notice. If you don't notice, then you might hire someone who is very bad at her job when you didn't mean to do that. I went and stood near one of the

assistants to see whether she was good or bad. She looked like someone I might like to hire someday. She was talking on the phone.

"We'll have a plan B," the assistant said. "Yes, a tent if it rains and two sets of vows. We always have a plan B, a backup plan, in case our first plan falls through."

That is when I knew this was a very good assistant. Never in my **worldwide life** did I know there was such a thing as a plan B. That is what the assistant taught me. I learned about a plan B, which is **a for instance** of something I did not know only four seconds ago in the past. I could not wait until this assistant worked for me.

And that's when I realized that there *could* be two wedding planners, **however and nevertheless**. Susan, the plan A wedding planner, was helping Julie, and I would be the plan B wedding planner who helped Elliott! It was **geniusal**.

CHAPTER

When we got home, I went to my
room to start building my wedding
planning office. I looked around
and thought about what I should
do first. That's when I knew! I ran
down the hall and asked my dad if he
had a clipboard. He did **indeed and
certainly**. He gave it to me and I ran
back to my wedding planning office.
Now I needed to clomp the clipboard
with wedding business. Clipboards

should never be empty. **That is a scientific fact and also the law.** Since I didn't have anything to clomp down on, I ran back down the hall to my parents' room.

"Do we have any magazines that I can cut up?" I asked my mom.

She pointed to the pile on the floor next to her desk. "You can have all of those," she said.

"Thanks!" I said and picked up the whole bunch.

In my office, I cut out the pictures that looked **weddingish** and filled my clipboard. Next, I needed to pin **weddingish** things onto my corkboard. But I didn't have any **weddingish** things like that. I ran all through my house to see if there was any little scrap of fabric I could use. I found a paper napkin, which I decided was very good. I tacked that to my board. I sat back and looked at my beautiful wedding planning office. The only thing it needed was assistants. My office wasn't big enough for **twentyteen** assistants. That's why I decided I'd hire just one assistant for now. I was going to hire Elliott. I called him, so he would

know about his new job.

"Elliott?" I asked when he picked up the phone.

"Hi, Frannie," he said.

"Tomorrow at lunch, can you have a meeting with me?"

"Sure," he said, **excitified**. "About what?"

"You're going to be my plan B wedding assistant!" I told him.

"Oh wow! But I'm already best man. I don't think I can have two jobs!"

"Yes, you can. The job is all about helping you be the best at being the best man. Don't worry. I'll explain everything. But don't schedule any other meetings for lunch tomorrow, okay?"

"I won't," he said. Then added, "I promise."

When we hung up, I was smiling all

the way from one side of my town to the other. That's how much I could not wait to get to work as a plan B wedding planner.

At dinner that night, I asked my parents what the best man did at a wedding. I listened very carefully to the answer because I didn't have paper or a pencil. What they said exactly was a lot. So much, my face almost **plopped** down into my vegetable soup.

"Well, at a traditional wedding, which Julie and George are not having," my mom started, "the best man has to make sure the groom has the marriage license."

"A license?" I asked.

"That's right," my dad said. "You need a license to get married."

"I did not know about that fact," I told them.

"Sometimes a best man helps the groom pack for his honeymoon and dress for the ceremony," my mom said.

"The best man also has to make sure the rings are safe and secure. He has to keep track of the vows. He has to keep track of everything, actually. He's almost like the groom's assistant," my dad told me.

I nodded my head at this.

"Sometimes a best man arranges for all the travel and the honeymoon. He makes the reservations, gets the tickets, buys traveler's checks," he continued.

"At the actual wedding, he makes sure that no one is dillydallying around," my mom told me. "And, he makes the first toast at the rehearsal dinner and at the wedding. He introduces people to one another so they all feel welcome."

"He also has to sign the marriage certificate," my dad added.

"Now, the maid of honor . . . ," my mom started, but I could not even remember what she said because my brain was about to **explode itself** into bits from all that information. That was too many jobs for anyone to do. I was starting to realize Elliott really needed a lot more help than I thought.

Before I went to bed that night, I cut up a tissue box to make brand-new business cards.

MRS. FRANKLY B. MILLER
PLAN B WEDDING PLANNER
CEO and DR

The next day, after twelveteen years of morning classes, it was finally lunchtime. Elliott and I ran downstairs to find a good meeting table. We sat down at four different ones until we found the exact right table for a business meeting. We left our backpacks on the table so no one would steal our spot. We got our lunch, came back with our trays of tacos, and got right down to work.

"Good afternoon, and welcome to this meeting," I announced to just Elliott. I reached into my back pocket and handed him my new business card. He studied it for a long time, which was something I **appreciated**.

"Thank you. Good afternoon," he said back, taking a big bite of his taco.

"Today is the meeting about best men and plan B wedding planners. You are already the best man. Now you will also be the assistant to the president of plan B wedding planners, Mrs. Frankly B. Miller," I told him.

He nodded, because his mouth was full.

"It is a scientific fact that I found out what a best man does, exactly. I will tell you that very **soonly**. But first, does everyone here know what a plan B is?" I asked him, knowing he did, but really wanting to explain it, anyway.

He nodded his head. His mouth was still full.

"What a plan B is, exactly, is when things go wrong and you have to do something else instead. The something else instead is a plan," I told him, even though he already knew about this fact.

Elliott nodded again. His mouth wasn't still full, he just really likes nodding.

"What we need now exactly is a plan B for this wedding. Everyone will get a plan B type of job," I told him.

"But I already have a plan *A* job," Elliott said.

"I know that, but you need to have a plan B job in case everything in your plan A job goes wrong," I said. "The most important thing is the license."

"The license?" Elliott asked.

"Yes, the best man has to learn how to drive because he needs a license or else the man and woman can't get married."

"But I'm not old enough to get a license!" he shouted.

"I know. I am worried about that, too," I told him.

That's when we both **scrunched up** our faces to think about a plan B about the license.

"Okay, we'll come back to the license. Let's talk about what you'll do if you lose the rings," I said.

That is when Elliott's face almost fell off.

"The rings?! What do I have to do with the rings?"

"You are the best man, Elliott. You are in charge of the best things! Everyone in the **worldwide of America** knows that wedding rings are one of the best things of a wedding."

"But I don't have the rings. George has them," Elliott told me, starting to scrunch up his hands in worry.

"Well, you have to get them because the rings are your job as best man."

"Okay," Elliott said. "I'll try and get them."

"Okay. Next we have to talk about the weather," I told him.

"The weather?"

"Yes. The wedding is outside, so you have to make sure it doesn't rain," I explained.

That is when Elliott stood up. "How in the world will I ever do that?" he nearly shouted.

I shrugged. "But you better figure it out because you're the best man. You're in charge of the weather. I'll try and find a lot of umbrellas," I said, writing that down. "Now, the honeymoon . . ."

"The honeymoon?" Elliott nearly fell over.

"Yes, you have to get them a honeymoon," I told him.

"I don't really even know what that is!" he cried.

I shrugged again. "Also, a speech and the vows."

"What about them?"

"You have to make them and write them."

"ALL of them?" he asked.

I nodded, taking a bite of my taco. When I chewed and swallowed I said, "Don't worry, Elliott. None of it is as hard as it sounds." Then I added, "Probably," because I was not sure that was a scientific fact.

CHAPTER

After school, Elliott came over because we had a lot of work to do. We had to write the vows, just in case George and Julie forgot to do it themselves. These were our plan B vows, and they were going to be **fantastical**.

I knew a lot about vows because I once read a wedding announcement in the newspaper, and it mentioned vows in the article. Plus, I've seen some

movies where people get married, and
I know about the things they say. We
brought my dog, Winston Churchill,
with us and sat in my wedding
planning office. I pulled out a legal pad.
It's a legal pad because it's for lawyers.

Elliott and I stared at each other,
stumpified.

"How does it go again?" Elliott asked
me.

"I know it starts with the name.
Like, 'I, Julie Stephenson, take you—'"
and that's when I remembered all of it.
I rushed it out fastly before I forgot it or
Elliott could interrupt me.

JULIE'S VOWS TO GEORGE:

I, Julie Stephenson, take you,
George Johnson, to be my awful
wedding husband on this day

forward for now and for worse, for Richard and the pourer, until death tears us into parts. I promise to love and to weigh you, whether you like it or not. You may now forever hold your peach. Almond.

GEORGE'S VOWS TO JULIE:

I, George Johnson, agree with you, Julie Stephenson, and take you to be my awful wedding wife on this day forward, for now and for worse, for Richard and the pourer, until death tears us into parts. I promise to love and to weigh you, whether you like it or not. You may now forever hold your peach. Almond.

Even though they were the only vows I'd ever read, I thought they were really **spectacularish**. Elliott agreed and felt very **relieviated** that that part was over.

"I think we should practice the wedding now," he said.

"That's a good idea," I told him.

"Because if anything goes wrong right now, we'll be able to fix it before it really happens!" he said.

I thought this was very **geniusal**.

"I don't want to put on the flower girl dress, though. Can Winston Churchill wear it and play my part?"

Elliott shrugged, which meant "I don't see why not."

I went to my closet and pulled the dress down off its hanger. It is very hard to put a dress on a dog, just in case you don't already know this. First, you have to put it over its head, which it does not like even for one second. Once you have that done, you have to lift each paw and put it through the sleeves, which it does not like, either. Then you are done! Once Winston Churchill had the dress on, we told him

to walk down the aisle. But, instead of doing that, he raced out of my bedroom!

"OH NO!" I yelled. "Winston Churchill, come back!" Elliott and I raced after him. My mom popped her head out of her bedroom.

"What's going on?" she asked.

"Nothing!" I yelled as I raced down the stairs and Elliott followed.

I heard the screen door slam shut, and Elliott and I stopped in our tracks to look at each other with "this is a very bad situation" eyeballs. When we got outside, I **gaspified**. Winston

Churchill, in my dress, was splashing around in a big mud puddle. Elliott and I raced to the puddle to pull him out. We dragged Winston Churchill to the screen door, which my mom was holding open for us. She had a very **angrified** look on her face, which gave me a very bad day feeling on my skin.

"Is Elliott in trouble, too?" I asked. "Or just me?"

"Just you," my mom said.

That is when my mom taught me how to do laundry all by myself. **Apparently and nevertheless**, I am very good at it because when the dress dried, it didn't look like anything bad had happened to it at all! It did shrink a little bit, but that was okay because it was too long to begin with. By the time Elliott's mom came to get him, I felt like we had gotten a lot done. We wrote the vows, and I learned how to do laundry. I also got in trouble, but that is a different story.

CHAPTER

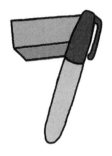

Before we even knew it, it was one entire day away from being the wedding. Things were getting very busy. Since I was the plan B wedding planner AND the flower girl, I had to be involved in every single thing leading up to the wedding. That is why I went with Julie, Elliott, my mom, and Jessica, Julie's sister, to the apple orchard where Julie and George were getting married. Susan, the plan A wedding planner, was meeting us there.

Jessica was the maid of honor. My job was much better than hers because mine had the word *flower* in it. *Flower* is a much fancier word than *maid*. Also because I was the person who came out right before the bride. My mom was in charge of the table decorations, which was a very big job. This meant she also had to do things with flowers. Since *flower* was in the title of my job, I knew she would need help. This was not a problem whatsoever. I went to a flower-arranging class once in my life, so I know all about flowers. This was going to come in handy for my mom. I couldn't wait to give her some helpful advice.

The orchard was a very beautiful place, indeed. My mom thinks of everything, so she brought two baskets for me and Elliott. We would pick apples while Jessica, Susan, my mom, and Julie did some wedding things. They didn't know that I was the plan B wedding planner, so that is **a for instance** of why I was not invited to join them.

Elliott and I went into the orchard, climbed a couple of trees, and picked the **bestiest** apples of forever. Then we decided to put the apples right at the place where Julie and George would be getting married because apples are very beautiful. We found the spot and tucked about twenty apples into the grass all around the special spot. When we were done, I looked around and felt a very big **ball of wonder** swell up inside me. How in the **worldwide of**

America were they going to decorate
the actual place of getting married?
How did a person decorate nature?

Elliott didn't have the answer to
this, either, but I had confidence that
we would figure it out. We went inside

the barn and found everyone gathered around talking.

"Are all the flowers here?" my mom asked Susan.

"Yes, they are all in the kitchen," she answered.

"Fantastic. May we go look at them?" my mom wanted to know.

"Of course," she said. "Follow me."

"Oh, this is so much fun!" Jessica said. I guess she had never seen flowers before.

We followed Susan downstairs to the kitchen part of the barn. Since the wedding was only one day away, people were getting the flowers ready. They were putting them in vases and filling them with water. There were so many vases to be filled, almost **twenty hundredteen**! Vases lined the table and counters, and there were even some on the floor. I was **horrendified** by this. **Apparently and nevertheless**, they did not know that flowers were supposed to be in the refrigerator! I know this because when I took my flower-arranging class, it was in a flower shop and all the flowers were in see-through refrigerators! I have always wanted a see-through refrigerator.

Susan said she was going to take Julie, Jessica, and my mom outside to look at the dining space and if we wanted to go outside we could join them. But I grabbed Elliott's hand and pulled it to tell him to stay put. When they left, I explained that we were about to save the entire wedding.

"How?" he asked.

"Apparently and nevertheless, no one knows that the flowers should be in the refrigerator! They're going to die if they stay out here like this," I said.

"Wow. I didn't know that," he said.

"I know," I told him. "It's a very good thing there is a plan B wedding planner."

We opened the refrigerator, which was very big and silver, and took the flower bunches out of their vases and laid them on their backs on the shelves. When we were done, we shut the refrigerator and washed our

flowered hands. I looked around the kitchen at all the empty vases of water and felt very proud indeed of our very good job.

When we were done at the orchard, we went to a makeup store. Jessica was going to do Julie's makeup for the wedding and had to learn how. Since I was the plan B wedding planner, I had to study the makeup part very carefully. If something happened to Jessica, I would know what to do.

Even if I don't care about or know how to use makeup, I look like a person who would know how to do something like that. I watched very carefully when the lady decorated Julie's face. When she was done, it didn't really look like she had much makeup on at all. I knew

that she was going to need my help.
Then the lady said, "If you want more,
just layer on more blush. If you want
less, you can dab it off with a napkin."

Easy. That's the exact thought I had.

"Now you try," the makeup lady said
to Jessica, who was so excitified that
she was getting to decorate Julie's face,
too. I felt a lot of **jealousification**
about that. When she was done, the
makeup lady said she did a great job,
which I did not agree with. That is not
an opinion.

Next it was off to the hair salon.
Elliott sat in the front area looking
through the magazines. I paid very
close attention to the hair part. Just
in case I had to plan B this, too. I was
horrendified when I heard Julie tell
the hairdresser that my mom was

going to do her hair. I could tell that the hairdresser, like the makeup lady, did not like this fact. She looked over at me, and I nodded to let her know that I understood and agreed with what she was telling me. She was telling me that I looked like a natural at hair and makeup, especially on wedding days.

However and nevertheless, the hairstyle was very complicated. There were a lot of twirls and loops and knots. Then they said something about flowers and putting them all over her hair. They said the flowers could be picked right from the apple orchard on the day of the wedding. That was a very exciting job to have. Since I knew about flowers, I decided that would be my job.

By the time we got back to the

car, my brain had almost **rinsed** the complicated hairstyle away. That made me a little **worrified**. But I could just make up my own hairstyle. I was very good at thinking on my feet. Even my dad says so.

CHAPTER

Before a wedding there is something called a rehearsal dinner. This is when the grown-ups eat dinner and make toasts and the kids get bored.

I don't know why it's called a rehearsal dinner because we did not practice eating dinner. What we did actually was *eat* dinner. Doing the thing is very different than practicing doing the thing. And that is a scientific fact.

I had to get dressed up for the rehearsal dinner, which was not something I preferred. I did not like having to dress up two times in one weekend! The dinner was at the apple orchard, and when we got there, I **gaspified** at how beautiful it was. They had lanterns and hanging Christmas tree lights twirled all over the place. Elliott was wearing a suit and looked very nice, but he did not like that he had to part his hair.

Susan, the wedding planner, told everyone in the wedding to come outside. We were going to rehearse the wedding! That's when everything started to make sense! First there was a rehearsal for the wedding, and then there was a dinner. They just put the two words together. There were people

I had never met before who were going to be the bridesmaids and groomsmen. They all seemed very nice.

"I'd like to do a very quick run-through before dinner," Susan said. Then she led George and Elliott to the very front. They were supposed to stand and wait for Julie. Elliott was disappointed that he didn't get to walk down the aisle, but when he learned he got to walk down the aisle at the end, he was happy.

"Okay," Susan called out to everyone. "We'll have Jessica and Brian walk down, then Anna and Dan, then Sarah and Paul," she said, pointing to the people I had never met. "Then Frannie, the flower girl, will walk down the aisle."

This was very excitifying. She

explained where the chairs would be and that we would walk in between them. She showed us where we would be standing. She showed us how to walk, too. It was a slow walk. You had to count to two at every step! Because I was the flower girl, I was going to have a big basket of flower petals to sprinkle on the ground. Susan showed me what that would look like. This was making

me very **can't-waitish**, indeed.

We all practiced the walk like Susan showed us. When we were all at the front, which is called the altar, she said, "And now the bride."

Julie was saving her special walk for the actual wedding. That is **a for instance** of why she didn't do the slow walk during the rehearsal. When Julie and George were both at the altar, Susan asked who would have the vows.

George said, "I'll have the vows in my blazer pocket."

I made a special note of this.

"Very good, and the rings?"

"We'd like Elliott to hold the rings," Julie said.

"Is that all right with you, Elliott?" George asked.

He nodded. He couldn't speak

because his mouth was too full with
pride-itity.

I smiled very hard at him, but then
my face hurt.

As the plan B wedding planner,
I was very glad to have all this
information. Now I knew all the plan
A plans. That meant I could do a plan
B for each of them. Once we had gone
through the whole ceremony, Susan
said we were done.

We went inside and found our
names on the place cards. There was
also salad on each person's plate! I liked
coming to a dinner where you didn't
have to worry about ordering.

In the middle of a hamburger bite, I
heard a **clinkety-clink** noise. Elliott
and I turned and saw that a man was
banging a knife against his glass!

That's when everyone got quiet and the man stood up. He started talking. That's when I realized that before a person gives a speech, they have to bang something against a glass! That made me love speeches even more! And I already really loved speeches!

After a few more people did it, I thought it was time for Elliott to make his speech. I nudged him in the side.

"You're the best man," I told him. "You have to make the best speech."

"But I don't have one! I don't know what to say!" he said, looking very **horrendified**, indeed.

"I'll whisper it to you," I told him. Before Elliott could even stop me, I was clanging a spoon against a glass and everyone got quiet. I nudged Elliott again, so he would stand up.

"Hi, my name is Elliott," I up-whispered to him.

"Hi, my name is Elliott," he said, looking down at me.

"Don't look down at me!" I ordered.

"Don't look down at me," he said.

I slapped my hand against my head. "No, I didn't mean for you to say that!"

Elliott swallowed and looked very pale.

"I am very happy that my mother is getting married to George."

"I am very happy that my mother is getting married to George," he said.

"Other than Frannie's mom—"

"Other than Frannie's mom—" Elliott copied.

"My mom is the best mom," I up-whispered.

"My mom is the best mom," he said.

Some people giggled a little bit. I don't know why.

"And George will be the best stepfather," I said.

"And George will be the best stepfather," he said.

"Thank you very much for your hospitality and good night!" I loud-whispered.

"Thank you very much for your hospitality and good night!" Elliott said and sat down, sweating into his fries.

George and Julie came over to us and gave us each a hug and kiss.

"That was a great team speech," Julie said to us.

We smiled because it was true.

CHAPTER

It was very **excitifying** to wake up and realize it was the day of the wedding! Even Winston Churchill was excited because he came racing into my bedroom. He was coming to the wedding with us.

My dad carried all our stuff to the car. Everyone was going to get ready in separate rooms at the barn. The boys in one room and the girls in the other.

When we got to the apple orchard,

we found Julie in the girls' room. She was in her bathrobe, and she was blow-drying her hair.

"You don't have to get dressed for a while, Frannie," my mom told me. "Why don't you go pick some flowers for Julie's hair?"

"Okay," I said, because I thought that was a **fantastical** idea. I raced downstairs and outside and saw Elliott climbing a tree.

"Elliott!" I yelled. "A best man isn't allowed to climb trees the day of the wedding!" Elliott did not know about this law apparently, He jumped down and ran toward me.

"Why not?"

"You might fall off and break something!"

"Good point," he said.

"I have to get flowers for your mom's hair," I told him. "Do you want to come and help me?"

"Yes!" he cried, and we raced toward the field. We collected the most beautiful flowers of ever. When we were almost done, I remembered we still had a couple things left to do.

"Do you have the rings?" I asked.

"Not yet. I have to get them," he said.

"Okay. And I have to give you the vows. You have to put them in George's inside blazer pocket."

"And then I hold the rings?" he asked me.

"No. You might lose them. We need a plan B for the rings."

We both **closed our faces**, so we could think for a little while.

Winston Churchill came running to us and jumped up when he saw Elliott. That was how **excitified** he was to see him.

"Winston Churchill!" I said. "We'll put the rings on his collar, so they won't fall off or get lost!"

"That is a very good idea, Frannie," Elliott told me. "Let's do that at the last minute, so that he's not running around with them before the wedding."

"Okay, good idea!" I told him. "Now, let's get the vows for you to put in George's blazer pocket. And get the rings. Don't forget to get the rings!" I ordered.

"Okay," he said. "I won't."

On the way to the girls' room to get the vows, we heard a big racket coming from the kitchen. Winston Churchill,

Elliott, and I ran to the kitchen. Susan, the wedding planner, was very upset. She was pulling the flowers out of the refrigerator. I thought it was a little too soon to do that.

"What's going on?" I asked.

"Someone put all the flowers in the freezer!" Susan yelled.

"You mean the refrigerator," I said.

"No, I mean the freezer! They're frozen solid!" she shrieked.

That's when I got a very bad day feeling on my skin.

"They're frozen!" Susan yelled again. "Frozen!"

Uh-oh.

Elliott and I ran out of the kitchen before Susan's head exploded. We raced upstairs to get the vows. When we got to the girls' room, I handed my mom the flowers and ran past her over to my bag. Elliott stood in the doorway, and when his mom came out of the other room in her bathrobe, Elliott got upset.

"Why aren't you in your dress? Did you forget that you're getting married?" he asked her, very **worrified**.

"Of course not!" she said. "I'm going to do my makeup first."

"Oh. Okay."

I handed him an envelope with the vows and whispered, "Put one in each pocket."

That's when Elliott smiled his **biggest smile of ever** at me. It was very good thinking on my part is what it was. I copied the vows five times, so that Elliott could put one into every single pocket of George's jacket, just in case George's got lost. That way, we didn't just have a plan B, we had plans C, D, E, F, and G!

I went over to Jessica, who was doing Julie's makeup. I had to make sure she was doing it correctly. If not, I'd have to jump in with some plan B makeup.

"That's a lot of blush. Do you think it's too much blush?" I asked.

"I don't think so," Jessica said, brushing Julie's cheeks.

"Also, don't forget about the eyes. And the lips. But don't make the lips too red. But, if you do, that's okay. I can probably fix them," I told her.

"Frannie!" my mom called.

"I'm helping Jessica do Julie's makeup!" I yelled back.

"Well, come help me with mine!" she yelled. It was hard to be needed in two places at once.

"I think I can handle it, Frannie. Thanks. When I'm done, you can have a good look," Jessica told me.

"Okay," I said, and raced over to my mother, who needed help only with getting zipped up, which was very boring, indeed.

Then it was my turn to get dressed. When I was done, I went back to look at Julie. I had to admit, she looked very beautiful. Even if I didn't really get to help her very much.

"You look so pretty," I told her.

"So do you," she said. "Now, who's going to help me get into my dress?"

"I will!" I shouted. I had never, ever helped anyone get into a wedding dress before. I felt very important, indeed. My mother and I held it open for her to step into, and we lifted it up to button all the buttons in the back. When we were done, we **gaspified** because she was so beautiful. Then it was time to do her hair.

My mom zipped her hands over Julie's head, **loop-de-looping** and **tunneling** flowers in different areas, and when she was done, Julie looked like the most beautiful bride I'd ever seen in the world.

My mom told me to go downstairs and get in position. She took Julie downstairs to the secret place they were going to hide before she walked down the grassy aisle. Before I went downstairs, I ran over to the makeup table and decided to make myself look just a little bit more beautiful. I put my fingers in the cream blush and rubbed it onto my cheeks until they were red. I put some red lipstick on, but I didn't like the taste, so I wiped it off with the back of my hand.

CHAPTER

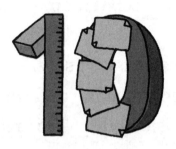

I ran downstairs to the apple orchard. There were a **millionteen** people sitting in chairs on two sides. Everyone was dressed up very beautiful and fancy.

Elliott came racing down the aisle toward me. He looked very nice, too.

"Did you put the envelope in George's blazer pocket?" I asked.

"Yes, and I have the rings, but I need your help putting them on

Winston Churchill's collar," he said.

We ran inside and found Winston Churchill. Elliott held him, while I unbuckled his collar, slipped the two rings onto it, and buckled it back up.

"That was easy," I said.

Elliott thanked me and ran back down the aisle and took his place.

My dad was calling for me from inside the barn. I rushed over to him, and he told me it was time to get into position. But first, he pulled out his handkerchief and wiped my face.

"Much better," he said when he was done **napkining** my face off. "Now get in line!"

My stomach filled up with moths and butterflies. I was so **nervousified**, I almost felt like I was the one getting married. When I turned around, I saw my mom. She came and stood in front of me in line. She had a huge smile on her face. Susan came up and handed me my basket of petals. They were like potato chips. That's how hard they were. My mom looked down at them and then up at Susan.

"They froze!" Susan told her.

"How?" my mom wanted to know.

"Someone put them in the freezer!" she said. "We're trying to defrost the others in time for dinner!"

Susan handed her the frozen bouquet. My mom had to keep switching hands because the flowers were **freezing her hands off**. Soon my dad came and stood next to my mom. Everyone was in place!

The people who were going to violin us down the aisle stood and started to ice-skate their bows across the strings. That was our cue to walk. Jessica and Brian walked first, followed by my mom and dad, and then Sarah and Paul. Then it was MY turn! I started my very slow walk and dipped my hand into the freezing petals. I sprinkled them onto the grass and they all landed with little *pfftt* sounds. I felt very important, indeed. Even though they were frozen, I thought I was making a very beautiful path for Julie. When I got to the front, I stood next to my mom. Winston Churchill was lying on the grass in the front row at someone's feet—in the **exact right** position for us to get the rings.

Then everyone in the audience stood up and turned to look at Elliott's mother and her father. She was the most beautiful bride in the **worldwide of America**. She wasn't wearing any shoes, which made me think she forgot. I almost jumped up to say something when I remembered that she wasn't planning on wearing shoes because of the grass! I always know when to keep my mouth shut.

Julie took a few steps and then sort of jumped. She looked down at the petals. I guess they were pretty cold. Julie and her father kept walking, but she made sure to step around the petals. It was funny.

When they reached us, George lifted the veil off Julie's face and whispered to her, "You look so beautiful."

"And you look very handsome," she whispered back.

Then they turned their backs to the audience, and we all sat down. The marrying man opened a book and started **boring everyone's faces off**. Soon I noticed Julie was getting **fidgety** in her legs. She kept lifting one foot to brush it against the other. That's when I remembered about our apples. I looked to see if I could spot them, and when I found them, I got a **very bad day feeling** on my skin. They were all brown and had holes in them. I sent a **brain note** to Elliott, but he was paying too close attention to the wedding and didn't receive it.

The marrying man asked them to bow their heads, so he could touch their head tops. This was a very weird wedding.

When they looked down, Julie jumped. And screamed, "Worms! Worms! There are worms everywhere!" She skittered away, while people stood up to see what was going on.

George and the marrying man looked down, and Elliott and I looked down, and sure enough, there were worms slithering all over the grass and into the apples. The **bad day feeling** on my skin got even worse.

"Worms are a very good omen," George yelled out to the audience. They laughed, and then George had a **geniusal** idea to move over a few feet, which is a for instance of what we did.

Once we were all settled in our new spot a few feet away, Elliott and I sent a fast bunch of **brain notes** back and forth about how we felt bad about the worms.

The marrying man said, "Your vows, please."

George reached into his pants pocket and pulled out the vows. He handed a piece of paper to Julie and kept one for himself. George had told us his vows would be in his blazer pocket. That's why Elliott put the plan B vows in his *pants* pocket. His pants pocket was the place for the plan B vows, and now George was going straight for the plan B vows, not plan A!

CHAPTER 11

Elliott and I looked at each other with "Why did he pull out the plan B vows instead of the plan A vows?" looks. Had George switched pockets and we didn't know?

Julie went first.

"I, Julie Stephenson, take you, George Johnson, to be my awful wedding husband," she began. "Wait, what is this? These aren't my vows!"

George looked down at his, read

them to himself, and burst out laughing. "These aren't my vows, either, but they're pretty funny."

"Where are the vows, George?" Julie asked, very **worrified**.

"Do you have them memorized?" the marrying man asked.

"I do," Julie said.

"I do," George said.

"Not yet!" someone yelled from the audience, and everyone laughed. They were joking about saying "I do" when it wasn't even time!

"They're in your blazer pocket," Elliott told George, who looked very **confusified**. He reached his hand into his blazer pocket and sure enough, he pulled out the plan A vows.

"How'd they get there?" George asked Elliott, who opened his mouth, but got cut off before he could answer. "You know what? Let's discuss this later. I'm getting married now."

Their vows were very beautiful, indeed. They had words like *respect* and *admire* and *love* and *nurture*. Very **adultish** words that I had to remember for my next wedding. But I felt a little **disappointment puddle** at my feet that they didn't read mine.

Then the moment we were waiting for arrived.

"May I have the rings, please?"

Everyone turned to Elliott, and at the same time, he and I both darted at Winston Churchill. I guess he got **alarmified** because he jumped up and barked. This was not something he normally did. As Elliott and I went toward him, Winston Churchill took off running.

"The rings!" Elliott shouted. "The rings are on Winston Churchill's collar!"

My dad and George followed after us.

Inside the barn, a tuxedoed man was rolling out a table. On top of it sat the most beautiful and biggest wedding cake I had ever seen in my life. He was pushing it to the middle of the room. Winston Churchill was running right toward it.

"Watch out! Watch out!" someone yelled. "The cake!"

The tuxedoed man saw Winston Churchill coming and froze.

"Move the cake, move the cake!" George was yelling, but the tuxedoed man did not move, and Winston Churchill was going right for it. George was the fastest runner in the **worldwide of America** because

one second before Winston Churchill
reached the table, George scooped him
up. That's when everyone clapped.
George put Winston Churchill down,
and Elliott helped hold the dog while
George took the rings off his collar. He
looked very out of breath.

When George held the two rings

up in the air, everyone hooted and hollered and **applausified** for George. I was very happy that he had saved the cake and the day, but I wished that it had been me. I like to save the day as **oftenly** as possible.

We went back to our places and

the wedding continued. The marrying man said a lot of words that sounded a lot like my vows. George and Julie repeated the vows while putting the rings on each other's fingers.

Then the most **excitifying** part came.

"I now pronounce you man and wife," the marrying man said.

And then the worst part.

"You may now kiss the bride."

Everyone stood up and cheered and clapped. The violin players stood and played a lively and fun walking-back-down-the-aisle song. Elliott's mom was married!

CHAPTER

Then it was time for the dance
and dinner! People who weren't at the
rehearsal dinner were going to make
some speeches, too. Even though I was
at the rehearsal dinner, I did not make
a speech. That is why I decided that
flower girls make speeches at wedding
dinners. A wedding dinner speech is **a
for instance** of something I planned
on making.

We went inside the barn where the

tables were all set up very beautifully with candles and hanging paper lanterns. The flowers were all in their vases. They were frozen and standing up extra tall, but they still looked very nice. Everyone thought so, not just me. Fancy tuxedo people came out with trays of champagne that they gave everyone. Elliott and I drank sparkling apple juice.

There was a *clink-clink-clink* sound. A woman started to talk about Julie and George. It was a very boring speech. There were other people who clinked and spoke. I really wanted to make that clinking sound again. As soon as the last boring speech was over, I tapped the side of my glass with a spoon, and the most beautiful clinky chimes came out of it. Everyone turned to look at me. I flushed right up with **hotness**, but then I started to make my speech.

"Hello, everyone. Thank you for coming to this wedding. It is not my wedding"—that's when everyone laughed, even though it was **a scientific fact** and not a joke—"but I am very happy that Julie and George got married. They met at my very

own house, which means that if our house had never been built, they never would have met." This was another **scientific fact** that they laughed at. "I would also like to say that if anyone else is going to get married soon, I am a professional wedding planner and"— everyone laughed so hard again, at another **scientific fact**—"I have a résumé and business cards . . ." I tried interrupting the laughter, but it was useless. Finally, I just said good-bye and **slunked** back toward Elliott.

The speeches were over and music started to play. My parents came over to me and Elliott. They **congratulated** Elliott because that's what you are supposed to do at a wedding. Then they asked to speak with me alone. This is not a good sentence.

"Whose idea was it to put the rings on Winston Churchill?" my dad asked in a strictish sort of voice.

"Mine?" I asked.

"And who wrote those vows and put them in George's pockets?" my mom asked me.

"Well, I wrote the vows, but Elliott put them in the pockets!"

"Did you tell him to do that?" my dad asked.

"Yes, but I'm the plan B wedding planner! I'm in charge of all the backup plans."

My parents looked at each other with smile faces in their eyeballs. Then they turned back to me.

"Where did you get that idea?" my mom asked.

"From Susan's office. I heard one

of the assistants saying that every wedding has a plan B. Just in case the rings or the vows go missing or it rains . . . ," I explained.

"Were you also the one who put the flowers in the freezer?" my mom asked.

"I didn't know they were going to freeze! I thought I put them in the refrigerator, like at the flower shop."

"We know that you like to be involved in things, Frannie, but this was not *your* wedding. You were too involved," my dad said.

"People should be involved only when they are asked—"

I opened my mouth to say something.

"—and not when you THINK someone MIGHT ask you," my mom said, reading my brain exactly.

"You need to apologize to Julie and George for all the trouble you caused," my dad told me. Then, "Speak of the devil!"

My mom and I looked up to see Julie, George, and Elliott coming over to us.

My dad nudged me.

I looked up at Julie and George. "I'm very sorry that I ruined your lives," I told them.

They laughed and George said, "You did no such thing."

"There were a lot of bumps and mishaps, that's for sure," Julie said. "But every wedding has its crazy moments, and these are ones we will remember and laugh about for years to come."

"Well, I'm sorry, anyway," I told

them. "I just wanted everything to be the best because Elliott was very worried about being the best man. I just wanted to help him!"

"You're a good friend, Frannie," George said. "Now let's go eat dinner. I'm starving!"

I turned to Elliott. "What happened with the vows?"

"George changed his mind about which pocket he was going to keep them in and didn't tell me! So when I found his vows in his pants pocket, I moved them to the top pocket of his blazer because that's where he said they'd be!" Elliott cried, still upset **apparently and nevertheless** that George had not told him about the change in pockets.

"Everything turned out okay, Elliott.

Don't be upset about it," I told him.

"I'll try," he promised. Elliott ran to the table, and while I was on my way, my parents stopped me.

"We have a lot more to discuss, you know," my mom told me.

This is **a for instance** of something I was afraid she'd say.

"I know," I told her.

"But now is not the time," my dad said. "When we get home. Now go find your seat, and let's eat some dinner."

I found my seat next to Elliott, and instead of hamburgers we had steak! Dinner was very loud and very fun. The band started to play and people were dancing. Elliott danced with his mom and I danced with my dad. I put my feet on my dad's feet and he lifted them, which made me dance. Then

Elliott danced with my mom and I danced with George. It was the most fun of ever.

Then, the band did a big drumroll, and the cake was wheeled over to George and Julie. They cut the cake together and fed each other a bite, which people say is romantic, but I think is **disgustifying**. My mom told me that some couples push the cake into each other's faces, which is a for instance of something I would not like to have done to me. The cake was wheeled away. My dad explained that there were professional cake cutters in the kitchen who were going to cut it so everyone got a slice when it was time for dessert.

Julie stood on the dance floor and yelled about catching the bouquet. I didn't know what that meant, but all the women jumped up and rushed over to the stairs. A lady I did not know grabbed my hand and raced me over there. Elliott wasn't allowed because he is a boy. As Julie climbed the stairs, I asked the lady next to me, "What is this even all about?"

"If you catch it, it means you will get married next. None of the girls right here are married yet, so we all want to catch it," she explained.

"Oh," I said. "I don't want to get married yet. I'm too young."

"Well, then back up so I can catch it," she said. I walked away as I heard Julie yelling, "One . . . two . . ."

I was out of the circle when she said *three*. I turned around because I wanted to see who caught it. She had

thrown it really far because when I looked up, it was coming right at me. I didn't know what to do except reach my arms up, and when they were up, I felt the soft *cooosh* of the bouquet.

I stared at it while everyone around me laughed and clapped. Except for the huddle of women who did not look too pleased. I will tell you for **a scientific fact** that I do not want to get married anytime soon. That is why I turned around and threw it back up into the air toward the women.

They all screamed and yelled, and the woman who wanted it the most caught it. That was who I was aiming for. She was so happy. She was jumping up and down holding the flowers and her eyes had tears in them. I knew when she looked at me with **"thank**

you" eyes that I would probably be her wedding planner. Her plan *A* wedding planner.

When the cake was served, Julie and George came over to sit with Elliott and my parents and me.

"We couldn't have done this without your help," Julie said to us.

"Thank you all so much," George said. "For everything. Especially for inviting us both to the same party so that we could meet each other!"

"You are very welcome," I said. "Even though I am in a **worldwide** of trouble, this was the most **funnest** wedding of the entire world," I told them.

"It really was," Elliott agreed.

"We think so, too," Julie told us. Then she looked right at me. "Do you want to read the vows you wrote out loud to your parents?" she asked.

I looked at everyone, smiled, and said, "I do."

THE END.

What is your favorite job that Frannie has tried her hand at?

Radio Show Host?

Frannie's class is visiting the local radio station and the host is nowhere to be found. Frannie decides she should cover for him. But what happens when listeners call in with questions and Frannie doesn't know the answers?

Veterinarian?

While visiting her aunt, Frannie decides to take her aunt's limping dog to the vet, who will be so impressed, he'll *have* to hire her. Will Frannie's doggy day care scheme succeed, or will it end in doggy disaster?

Food Critic?

When Frannie's parents take her to a new French restaurant, she discovers a new job: food critic! But if the restaurant is as fancy as it's supposed to be, why in the wide world of America are they serving SNAILS?

Keynote Speaker?

Frannie and her family are on vacation! But Frannie is more interested in what is going on in the hotel—a business conference—than theme parks! What happens when Frannie thinks she knows best for the keynote speaker?

School Principal?

Frannie wins the job of Principal for the Day! She even gets to hold her own assembly—that is, *if* she can stay out of trouble all day. As principal of her own school, does she get to come up with her own punishment?

Fashion Designer?

Frannie is in a mother-daughter fashion show! Mrs. Miller can't wait—but Frannie feels that being a designer for the show would be much more workerish than modeling. Can Frannie find a way to shine?

Fortune-Teller?

Frannie's parents throw a party, and she finds her next new job: fortune-teller! Frannie begins making up the fortunes of her friends at school . . . but what happens when her friends take things too seriously?

Rock Star?

When Frannie's local recreation center announces it's going out of business, Frannie and her friends join together to create a fund-raising concert! Being a rock star is the perfect career . . . or is it?